I headed straight for my bedroom and quietly clicked the door shut. Then I wheeled over to my dresser and stared into the mirror. It wasn't easy to find the real me through the photos, stickers, and pictures of horses tucked in the mirror frame. But there I was—long brown hair with the frizzy edges of a leftover permanent, a pug nose with a smattering of light freckles, and true blue eyes. They weren't hazel or gray, but blue. Probably the best thing I've got going for me. It's funny—I've only started thinking about my eye color as a plus this year. No doubt more pressure brought on by junior high.

I got bored with the mirror, so I pulled open the top dresser and lifted my Box—a large, cream-colored one with an embroidered flip-top lid—onto my lap. A lot of kids write in their diaries, but I've never been one to do things just like everyone else. I write to my Box.

To: Ambrelee Marie Primrose
From: Grandpa & Grandma Felabom; We love you!

Christmas 1988

DARCY

JONI EARECKSON TADA

Chariot Books
David C. Cook Publishing Co.

Chariot Books is an imprint of David C. Cook
Publishing Co.
David C. Cook Publishing Co., Elgin, Illinois 60120
David C. Cook Publishing Co., Weston, Ontario

DARCY

Cover illustration by Ann Neilson

First printing, 1988
Printed in the United States of America
92 91 90 89 88   1 2 3 4 5

Library of Congress Calaloging-in-Publication Data

Tada, Joni Eareckson.
  Darcy.

  Summary: Although she has come to terms with her
handicap and is adept at using her wheelchair, Darcy
is worried and nervous about going to junior high
school and turns to God for help.

  [1. Physically handicapped—Fiction. 2. Schools—
Fiction. 3. Christian life—Fiction] I. Title.
PZ7.T116Dar 1988   [Fic]   87-35712
ISBN 1-55513-809-8

To Ricky, Shawn, Kelly,
Kay, and Earecka—
special children
who helped me
the most.

1

Willowbrook in summertime is a wonderful place to be. At least it always has been.

That Thursday everything looked different ... yet the same. The shady road that borders the back of Willowbrook Elementary School and leads to our neighborhood is lined with exactly twenty-five maple trees and three different kinds of picket fences. When you turn right at the entrance to our housing development, it's best to walk in the road because the sidewalk is ruined with a zillion bumps and cracks. That's probably because Chipper has been kicking pebbles there for years every time we walk back and forth between school and home.

One block up, you pass a yellow house where a friendly bulldog lives. Next door is a gray two-story where a fiesty old Siamese cat makes his home. Mandy always stops and gives her lunch bag leftovers to those two. Go a little further and you pass an old orange fire hydrant, a favorite springboard for April's flying cartwheels.

Chipper, Mandy, April, and I have walked home this way jillions of times since we were little kids in kindergarten. Actually, I, Darcy DeAngelis, have to confess that I don't walk. I wheel my way from school to home. No, not on a bicycle—in a wheelchair.

I've always thought my wheelchair is as nifty a set of wheels as most of the suped-up bikes my friends own. It has a bright purple frame, whitewall tires, cartoon stickers on the sides, and black foam grips with purple and pink streamers on the handles. Actually, my wheelchair makes most bicycles look boring. But this day, even my wild and crazy wheelchair couldn't make things bright. This day was different.

I glanced at my friends. Mandy was twisting her blonde pigtails and cracking her gum. April was pretending the curb was a balance beam. Too-tall Chip was swinging his knapsack of books back and forth as he walked. Did they feel the same?

I threw out my question to nobody in particular. "Think you'll miss sixth grade?"

April hopped off the curb and pirouetted into the street. "No way. I've had my fill of little kids; now I'm ready for the big time. What do you say, Chipper, ol' boy?" She leaped up on the curb as though practicing mounts for the balance beam.

Chip shrugged and kept swinging his books. I couldn't tell if he really didn't have an answer or was just trying to ignore April. She can be awfully obnoxious at times.

Then he said, "It'll be a relief to get out of Willowbrook and leave my two little brothers behind. Junior high," he continued, as if he were imagining himself as the big man on campus. "Seventh grade's no big deal —except maybe pre-algebra."

That's the kind of stuff that made me nervous about junior high. Dividing decimals is one thing, but seventh grade pre-algebra? Aaagh! And how would I cope with Spanish when I've never made it past the first round of a spelling bee in English? And I had a feeling that junior high literature would be a lot

9

more complicated than last month's Weekly Reader.

Junior high. Not a bona-fide recess in there anywhere. Nobody collecting lunch money. No teachers, like substitute moms, digging into their purses to give you change for milk if you happen to forget. No Valentine's Day parties or parading around the playground in Halloween costumes. No more kid stuff—just seven different teachers for seven different subjects in seven different classrooms.

"I can't wait to try out for soccer!" Mandy said, following behind April on the balance beam curb.

"*I'm* going to join the drama club," April said.

That fit. Everything about April was dramatic. She was constantly preening her long red hair, knotting it into a bun one minute and French braiding it the next. If she wasn't doing that, she was tucking in her blouse, pulling up her knee-highs, or fluffing her sleeves. Anybody who paid that much attention to herself had a problem, as far as I was concerned.

"If not the drama club," she gushed, "then definitely cheerleading."

I began to feel a little left out.

April blabbed on. "Jordan Junior High is a big campus—isn't that the coolest word, *campus*? They make you change classes real fast. Everybody has to race to get to the next classroom on time. Sometimes kids get lost."

I'd heard that tone of voice before. I had a feeling April could care less about how big the school is. She just wanted to frighten Chipper and Mandy, and especially me. As I said, she can be obnoxious.

"How are *you* ever going to make it to class on time, Darcy?"

I sighed and rolled my eyes. "Super charged batteries, steel-belted radials, and mag wheel hubcaps." April cracked up, and I kept going. "With a super-charged breakfast of champions. . . . Yes, it's Wheaties, the number one official sponsor of the U.S. Olympic Team," I used my best Saturday morning television commerical voice. "Yes, kids, with 100% of the Recommended Daily Allowance you will build strong bodies twelve different ways. Tell your parents you want—Wheaties!"

April cartwheeled off the curb and onto the street again, giggling and losing her balance. That's the best way to handle April—just keep her laughing. I don't know why, but it's important to me that she not get all serious and morbid about my chair. Besides, April is one of those people who can't be serious without sounding like she's looking down her nose at you. It also doesn't help that she's about as deep as a paper towel.

Mandy strolled up behind me and leaned on the handles of my chair. "Seriously, Darce, have you thought about changing classes in junior high? Are you going to need help being pushed?"

Good old Mandy. She's always ready to push me up a steep hill, pick up my dropped books, or reach for our Nancy Drew favorites on the top shelf of the library—and all without sounding high and mighty about it.

"Naw," I said. "I'll just put a horn on my chair and honk my way from class to class." I crouched low and sped ahead, careening up on one wheel—my impression of an eighteen-wheeler barreling down the interstate.

"What a loony-tune," Mandy said, throwing a pebble after me. I coasted along while she and the others caught up.

The rest of the way home I savored the

sight of each tree we passed. Every bump in the sidewalk. Our bulldog friend who greeted us at his front yard gate and the Siamese cat who did his best to ignore us. Maybe Mandy and April and Chip weren't sad about leaving elementary school behind, but I sure was.

The four of us split up at the corner of my street, Chipper to head for swim practice, April to perfect her arabesques, and Mandy to work on her stamp collection.

"Catch you later," I yelled after them, wheeling toward my house. I looked back —we were all good friends, even though there were a few things we didn't like about each other. Would we still be friends in junior high? Would we have the same classes? Would I even *see* them in the halls?

I turned into our brick driveway. From this angle my house looked exactly like one of those drawings that second graders make—a white house with red shutters, complete with brick chimney and two bushes on either side of the front steps. In the six years I've been in elementary school, the bushes have grown taller than me. Of course, that could be because I'm so short sitting in this wheelchair.

I sucked in a deep breath. Even my own home looked different, now that I was a real, live graduate—even if it was only from sixth grade.

I started wheeling up the driveway and stopped. My little brother, Josh, had left his bike in my way again.

"Mo-o-m!"

My mother pushed the screen door open with her elbow while wiping her hands on a dish towel. "How many times have I told that boy to use the kickstand on this thing," she said as she tucked the towel under her elbow and wheeled the bike into the garage.

Neither of us was really upset at Josh —our whole family is used to making way for my wheelchair. I angled my chair toward the ramp at the side garage door.

"So how was your day, Darcy?" Mom asked as she gave me a shove up the ramp. We both knew I was being unusually quiet.

"Okay, I guess," I mumbled as I slung my empty bookbag off the handle of my wheelchair and plopped it on the kitchen counter. "We turned in our books. Paid some library fees. Passed around autograph books." I jerked open the refrigerator door for a snack. "Nothing special."

14

Mom gave me a look that means "you're not telling me the whole story." But I figured she was adult enough to know that kids have days like these. Life-changing days, when you leave behind one era and prepare to face a scary new world.

"Honey," she said as she tucked my bangs behind my ears, "don't be frightened about next fall."

How is it that moms can tell what's going on in a kid's head?

"Don't be worrying yourself about school, Darcy. Goodness, you've got an exciting summer ahead." She sat down across the table from me. "Family camp is in just a couple of weeks, and all your friends from church will be there."

She had a point there. Family camp was a bright spot on the horizon. I waited for the idea of camp to scare away my sad feelings, but the sadness stayed, so I decided to keep dwelling on the junior high horrors.

At dinner I pushed peas around on my plate while Josh blabbered on about the knots he was learning to make at Cub Scouts. Mom had to tell him three times to put down his napkin, which he had mangled into two square knots and a slip knot.

My older sister, Monica, who is always buying *Seventeen* magazine and calling boys on the phone, raved about her cute water safety instructor at the pool. I've wondered if he's the only reason she's working on her lifesaving certificate. Mostly, though, Monica is okay. She treats me and the rest of my friends like regular people.

But tonight I couldn't do much more than lean on my elbow, squish peas between my teeth, and listen to the others talk.

After dinner I didn't bother to watch TV with the rest of the family. Dad had popped microwave popcorn for the week's best night of sit-coms, but I just stopped by the living room to say good night. Monica and Josh gave each other a funny look—they knew I was passing up my favorite shows.

I headed straight for my bedroom and quietly clicked the door shut. Then I wheeled over to my dresser and stared into the mirror. It wasn't easy to find the real me through the photos, stickers, and pictures of horses tucked in the mirror frame. But there I was—long brown hair with the frizzy edges of a leftover permanent, a pug nose with a smattering of light freckles, and true blue eyes. They weren't hazel or gray, but blue. Probably the best thing I've got going for me. It's funny—I've only started thinking about my eye color as a plus this year. No doubt more pressure brought on by junior high.

I got bored with the mirror, so I pulled open the top drawer and lifted my Box—a large, cream-colored one with an embroidered fliptop lid—onto my lap. A lot of kids write in their diaries, but I've never been one to do things just like everyone else. I write to my Box.

2

The thing with the Box started back in second grade, when I landed in the hospital after an automobile accident. It wasn't the driver's fault—I darted on my bicycle into the street from behind a parked car. Next thing I knew I was flat on my back in an ambulance, sirens screaming.

That was a super scary time for me and my whole family. When my relatives and all the kids in school sent me tons of get-well cards, Mom kept their notes, along with newspaper clippings about my accident, in the cream-colored box. After visiting hours were over, I would lie on my side in bed and

18

thumb through all the letters and cards. That's when the box became "The Box."

I don't know how to explain it—that old box became a, well . . . a friend I could talk to. And a friend I could give things to— ticket stubs from favorite movies, a ring from my grandmother, a lace hanky from my roommate in the hospital children's ward. Does that make any sense?

When I came home from the hospital, most people stopped writing, but I had to stay forever in a wheelchair. I knew my relatives were 'tsk-tsking' and kids in school were scared to face me. I couldn't blame them. I probably would have said and done nothing, too, if it had been someone else. I guess people run out of things to say. You know, all those get-well cards . . . and yet I never really got "well." So the cards and notes stopped. But I kept adding things to my Box.

I parked my wheelchair up against my bed, lifted my paralyzed legs and propped them up on a pillow, and leaned back in my chair. I tapped my pen on my notepad, thinking.

Dear Box, I scrawled. *Have you ever felt different? I mean really different?*

Today was the last day of school. Everybody was super excited, like they were being released from prison or something. I joked around with everyone as usual, but underneath I wondered if my friends felt like I do . . . petrified.

Aril said something about changing classes. Well, that's not all I'm scared about. Suppose they assign me a locker that I can't reach from my wheelchair? Suppose I have a classroom on the second floor and there's no ramp or elevator? What if I can't fit in the bathroom? And I'll just die if the mirrors are too high above the sinks. All the girls will be gawking at themselves in a mirror, and I'll have to sit there like a jerk.

I double-clicked the top of my ball point pen. Words came much easier when I shared them with my Box.

And the more I pretend that I'm not scared, the scareder (is that a word, Box?) I get. I can't even tell Mandy how I feel.

Goodbye for now. Darcy.

I wedged the pen behind my ear and shifted my hips in the chair. My legs, limp and lifeless, shifted on the bed as I moved. They really weren't bad-looking legs. I had on knee-highs with tennis shoes. Some days

I wore sweat pants with running shoes. Other days Mom lets me wear pantyhose with my skirts. Occasionally, I've even painted my toenails. But no matter how much I dress them up, the fact is obvious—I can't move my legs. I can't even feel my toes.

I sighed and rummaged through my Box. There was the letter I had written last year after our gym class learned a bunch of square dances. I had to sit on the sidelines and run the record player, watching while everyone else do-se-doed with a partner. That was one day I couldn't come back fast enough with smart-aleck comments.

I spilled my guts to my Box that afternoon. I remember how I felt when I wrote —kind of teary and mushy, but in a good way. At the close of the letter, I was surprised to read, *"I will never leave you or forsake you. . . . I am with you always."*

I recognized that as a verse Monica had shown me from her Bible. It felt good to have my older sister give me something so private and personal as a favorite verse. Monica may have the appearance of being boy-crazy, but she's deeper than that. That verse about Jesus never leaving me had stayed with me for months—but that was

21

over a year ago. Reading it again made me feel a little sad. I haven't been as close to God as I should be.

Suddenly, I pushed the Box aside. It wasn't enough to write; I needed somebody to talk to. I wished Mandy were with me.

I grabbed my legs, plopped them back on the foot pedals, and quickly wheeled over to my closet. There, behind three pairs of shoes, a empty Coke can, and a lot of dust, lay Rabbie, my old stuffed rabbit. I gently picked him up and turned his dirty, worn out body over in my hands. He was missing an eye and had an ugly Coke stain on his stomach from lying so long at the bottom of my closet.

I beat some dust off Rabbie's backside. He's always had a lot of personality. I would die in a pile if somebody like April even heard me say such a thing, though I wouldn't mind if Chip or Mandy knew. In face, Mandy once told me, when we were having one of our sort-of-serious talks about God, that it was easier for her to talk to Jesus when she scrunched up against her special silk and lace pillow.

I looked Rabbie squarely in his one-eyed face and decided to try Mandy's way of praying. Praying. The word itself made me cling to Rabbie.

When I was a little kid in the hospital, I used to hold Rabbie tightly whenever I talked to God. Somehow it was comforting to think that Rabbie could listen in to whatever I was saying. But I got older and retired my rabbit, knowing that God was listening whether I held a stuffed animal or not. But lately, as I said, I haven't been as close to Him as I should.

I took a deep breath and began to pray. I couldn't believe the words that tumbled out of my mouth.

"It's just not fair," I blurted to God. Then I stopped a moment and cringed, as if I expected lightning to crash through my bedroom ceiling.

"I won't know anybody in junior high. April I can handle. Chipper I can cut up with. And most of the kids in my elementary school think I'm okay, because I can make them laugh about my wheelchair. But You know that it's taken me since second grade to get them to loosen up around my paralyzed legs. I don't think I can go through all that again in junior high, with hundreds of new kids who will think my brain is paralyzed just because my legs are!"

I breathed a big sigh of relief. I had finally told someone how I actually felt way down deep. And I did it without cracking a joke.

"Amen," I added.

I leaned my head against Rabbie, listening to the quiet. Maybe I was expecting a kind of Tony-the-Tiger voice to boom down from heaven and tell me everything was going to be okay. But the only sounds were muffled television voices drifting in from the living room.

I wheeled back to my bed and placed Rabbie on the side of my pillow. Although I had retired him long ago, with my Barbie doll collection and comic books, I felt he deserved to be back in the land of the living—at least for a night. And that night as I lay in bed, I held him the way I used to when I was little.

3

The next day, our first day of summer vacation, Mandy tromped over to my house, lugging her stamp collection. I edged out of my wheelchair and lowered myself onto the braided rug in my bedroom. I like being eye level with friends, especially when we're goofing off. Mandy and I spread out her stamps into rows of different countries and colors. For the first few minutes, we worked quietly.

I've always thought of Mandy as as an honest-to-goodness friend. That's partly because we've been best buddies since kindergarten. Then again, I've known April that long and I sure don't feel as close to her. Maybe it's because Mandy and I are on the same wavelength. We both like to read, study stamps, draw horses, play Parcheesi, talk about our feelings, and even daydream about boys every once in a great while.

I respect Mandy, too. She's brave enough to talk back to April, something I can't do. That's why I usually hide my feelings in a joke.

It's not that I'm afraid of April, although she *is* one of those kids who tend to run the show at school. It's just that I can't afford to get on the wrong side of her, because she sways everybody's opinion so easily. Maybe I am a little afraid of her. I've got enough problems handling my friendships from this wheelchair; I don't want to pile on extra headaches.

Mandy broke our comfortable silence. "Excited about family camp this summer?"

I picked up a stamp with Monica's eyebrow tweezers and carefully placed it in one of the rows. "I guess."

Mandy raised her head, threw back her pigtails, and leaned on her arm. "What's with you? Nothing gets you excited these days. Not even getting out of school."

26

"Not so," I answered, pretending I had no idea what she was talking about. I reached for another stamp.

Mandy sighed. "Seems to me you've been keeping a lot inside the last few weeks."

Having a best friend carries some built-in risks. Like moms, best friends have a way of knowing when something's wrong. And if they're *really* best friends, they won't let you rest until they dig it out of you.

I lay on my side and picked with the tweezers at a loose thread in the rug. "Remember how neat it was when we were together in first grade ... before my accident?"

"Yeah." Mandy grinned. "We were the terrors of Willowbrook. Remember that time we raced against the best girls in second and third grade?"

I'd never forget. That was one of those fun memories I kept crystal clear in my mind.

"We beat them all," she giggled. "Darcy, you were the fastest friend anybody ever had."

The silence came back again. The accident that paralyzed my legs happened just a couple of months after that.

"You were also the *best* friend anybody

could have," Mandy added.

"*Were?*" I said in an insulted tone, raising my eyebrows and folding my arms.

"Okay, okay. You still *are* my best friend." Mandy crossed her eyes and stuck out her tongue. Then she looked serious. "Although lately you seem to be covering up an awful lot. You know, all those wisecracks you make."

I started twisting all the loose rug threads together. Should I tell her? No way. If I told Mandy about my fears, she would really know what was going on inside of me. And then she'd expect me to *do* something about my stupid scary feelings. I decided to change the subject.

"Are you going to room with your family or with the junior high girls at camp?" I asked her, propping myself up against the side of my bed.

She paused, giving me a sideways glance. "Mom and Dad are letting me stay at the pre-teen cabin." Her tone of voice told me she knew exactly what I was up to, but she would let me get away with it.

"Me, too, I hope."

"We're going to follow you guys up to the mountains in our station wagon. I can't wait," she added with a big grin. "There'll be a watermelon-eating contest, and campfires, and a big volleyball tournament. I'm gonna try and make it on Chip's team. Er, that is, *we* could try," she said, lowering her voice.

"That's okay," I said with a shrug. "I know what you mean."

"Yeah, I know you do. What a jerk I am," she said, conking herself in the head. "You'd think after all we've been through, I'd watch my words."

"Rela-a-x. It's no big deal," I said to make her feel better. "I don't want you to have to watch your Ps and Qs around me."

I honestly didn't mind. If kids had to tiptoe around me everytime they wanted to say something, they'd never get over my wheelchair.

Mandy breathed a sigh of relief. "As I was saying, let's you and I get Chip on *our* volleyball team. He'd be super. Have you noticed how tall he's shot up lately?"

I had noticed. Chip was beginning to look like he would easily fit in junior high. He's almost thirteen, but he looks like he's already fourteen. I secretly wondered if Mandy was beginning to *like* Chip—you know, like more than just friends. But I told myself that she had her head on too straight to start thinking wierd thoughts about Chip, even if he is getting cute. I mean, we knew him in first grade when he got his sleeves crusty from wiping his runny nose all the time.

I shook that thought off quickly. "Yeah, we'll rotate him around the net. I'll stay the point man in the corner. My wheelchair might run over somebody's toes if I get out in the middle."

We both knew that the rules had to be bent a little bit to let me play in my wheelchair. In gym, I would stay in the corner position of the court and the rest of the kids would rotate around me. I might not be able to zoom across the court in my chair, but I have a pretty good reach if the ball comes close to me.

"Ha!" Mandy leaned back and laughed. "I can just see April with tire treads on those fancy new exercise shoes her mother bought her for. Yuck. Can you imagine a kid our age into aerobics?!"

I stifled a chuckle. Poor April. I held up the tweezers and began pretending I was plucking my eyebrows in a snooty way. "Oh yes. We must look perfect, mustn't we?" I snorted. I wanted to say some more rotten things about her, but I put a lid on it. Mandy and I knew we were being nasty.

Family camp sounded fantastic. Watermelon, volleyball, fishing—I couldn't wait. I even knew Pastor Rob's evening stories would be neat—he always loosens up when he gives talks away from church. But then again, I wondered if I'd be able to get around okay. Before I'd always stayed with my parents in their cabin. Suddenly I wished that God *would* tell me in a booming voice that everything would be okay.

Mandy and I finished off the morning talking about camp and Chip and volleyball, as we lazily picked and chose our stamps.

Mandy finished pasting the last one in her book. She glanced at her watch. "Yeow, I gotta get going!" she said, scrambling to her feet and tucking her book under her arm. "Mom said I had to be home for lunch."

I scooted myself over to my chair. As she'd done a hundred times before, Mandy stopped and gave me her hand. I grabbed on, she pulled, and together we lifted my backside onto the seat of my wheelchair.

31

"Man, you're strong, Darcy."

"Look . . . up in the sky! It's a bird. It's a plane. No, it's Super-Crip! Disguised as Darcy DeAngelis, mild-mannered student of Willowbrook School . . ." I trailed off. *There I go, trying to be funny again. And I don't even need to in front of Mandy.*

"I'm out of here." Mandy paused on one foot at the door. "Okay?" She brushed her bangs off her face.

"Okay," I said as I straightened the creases on my jeans. "Call me."

I heard Mandy race down the hall and slam the back door. I wheeled over to my window and watched her run. Yep, she was the fastest thing I knew on two legs. I grinned, thinking about that race in second grade. Suddenly, my stomach knotted and I found myself swallowing extra hard. Why? Why these stupid feelings? It was nothing new to see Mandy run.

But I made it through our entire stamp-pasting session without opening up and letting her know what was really going on in my head. I thought I'd feel glad.

Instead, I felt worse.

4

Dear Box,

Three weeks of summer are already gone. April has been in Cincinnati visiting her grandparents, and I can't say I've missed her, although it would have been fun to have more kids go with our family to Six Flags. We ended up taking Josh's Cub Scouts. Mandy and I landed the job of watching over them.

Little kids don't seem to mind my wheelchair as much as some adults who keep patting me on the head and telling me in a cutesy voice how brave I am. I wish those adults would grow up.

A little boy named Derek sat next to me on

33

the roller coaster. You should have seen his eyes bulge when my dad lifted me up out of my wheelchair and plopped me on the front seat. When I patted the space next to me for Derek to sit down, he stood there like his shoes were nailed to the floor. I guess he thought I never got out of my wheelchair.

Then—get this—he asked if I wanted to hold his hand. How cute! He must take his Cub Scout oath seriously. When I said, "Sure, I'd like to hold your hand," he told me he'd make sure I wouldn't fall out.

I shifted my pen into my other hand and shook out my arm. Writing to my Box was becoming a favorite summer pasttime. Soon I would need a larger box.

Derek had a ton of questions after we got off the ride, but they weren't morbid or anything. He wanted to look at the bottoms of my shoes to see if they were scuffed—he honestly thought I was faking. He wanted to know if I slept in my wheelchair. And then he started jabbing me, asking if I could feel this or feel that. When he saw Mom push me into the bathrooms, he really got curious. "You go to the bathroom?" he said.

"Yeah, don't you?" I jabbed him back and he got the giggles. From then on, he rode on

the back of my chair, asked to get me pop-
corn, and ran block for me through the
crowds.

I think maybe I want to work with kids
when I grow up—they are so cool.

Monica yelled that dinner was ready, and
I quickly stuffed the letter back into my
Box. I jammed it into my dresser drawer
and swung my wheelchair around toward
the hallway. This was one dinner I didn't
want to be late for. Tonight Dad promised a
family meeting about our trip to family
camp.

After pork chops and macaroni with
cheese, Josh and Monica quickly cleared the
table. Mom poured Dad a cup of coffee, and
we kids leaned on our elbows, ready to
listen.

"Here's the scoop," Dad began as he shuffled the registration forms. "We've usually
camped together as a family, but this year,
by popular demand, we're doing things a little differently. Monica, you'll be staying in
the teen cabin—"

"All right!" Monica slapped the table.

"But I want you to observe the rules,
young lady. Your mother's and my cabin is
just across the ravine, don't forget," Dad

said as he shook his finger.

Monica got one of her Chesire cat grins. Mom and Dad showed her a lot of trust, which she deserved, I thought, even if she was the best looking girl at church and was always getting phone calls from boys.

"Josh, are you sure you want to stay with your friends in the Woodchuck cabin?"

Josh nodded bravely. This would be a big step for him, being away from Mommy and Daddy. But that's what he wanted. That's what I wanted, too.

"And Darcy . . ." Dad tapped the forms into a neat pile. "You'll be staying with your mother and me."

"What?!"

At Dad's look, I softened my tone of voice. "But, Dad . . . Mom," I said, looking from one to the other. "Monica and Josh get to be with their friends. Why can't I?"

Dad explained that the pre-teen cabin wasn't accessible. The space between the bunkbeds was tight, there was no ramp, and the showers wouldn't allow a wheelchair. Their cabin, he pointed out, had lots of room.

"Yeah, I know why," I mumbled. "It's because your cabin was designed for old

36

people . . . in wheelchairs."

"Darcy," Dad started, but I interrupted.

"Even Josh gets to stay with his friends, and he's just a little kid!"

"Let's have a Feel-Sorry-for-Darcy Day," Monica said, trying to snap me out of it. Sometimes a comment like that can bring me to my senses, but I was pretty upset.

Mom stood up, walked over to my chair, and smoothed my hair. While Dad tried to make the whole idea sound appealing by reminding me that I could still take part in all the pre-teen activities, Mother began to braid the ends of my perm. She does that when she feels bad about my limitations.

"Okay, okay," I fumed. "I'll stay with you guys. But you know it isn't fair."

It was tough to sleep that night. I lay there wide awake, knowing Josh was snoozing in the next room and Monica was playing her radio underneath her covers. As if junior high wasn't enough to think about, now I had to worry about camp. Mandy and April and the rest of the kids would be having a blast without me.

I turned my head on the pillow and saw the shadowy outline of my wheelchair in the corner of my bedroom. In the dark, the chair didn't look as nifty and fun. It just looked different.

I thought about last Sunday's church service when Pastor Rob talked about how different we all are—some Christians are strong and some are weak. As he spoke, I couldn't take my eyes off those old nursing home people in wheelchairs who lined the aisles along the pews. Would that be me someday? Ugh—I didn't want to be *that* different!

Lying there in bed, I suddenly felt more handicapped than ever before.

The next afternoon I sat in our driveway, reading a Nancy Drew book. It wasn't grabbing me, though, and besides, the breeze was so strong it kept turning the pages. I wedged the book in between my leg and wheelchair.

Leaning back, I gazed at the clouds racing across the bluest sky I'd ever seen. *Junior high. Family camp. I'm sick and tired of worrying!*

Another breeze roared through the trees lining our driveway, so strong it almost took my breath away. Even my wheelchair rolled back slightly against the force of the wind. I felt as though I could be lifted up into the breeze like Dorothy in *The Wizard of Oz*. I felt as light as the air around me, as though a hundred helium balloons were tied to my wheels. What a beautiful feeling! I pictured myself jumping out of my wheelchair and dancing with the wind, letting my skirt whip wildly in the breeze. That's what I wanted to do.

But I couldn't. I tucked my billowing skirt underneath my lifeless legs and a flood of memories of what it was like to run and skip and dance came pouring over me. The wind died and so did my feelings—I didn't want to be different. I wanted to be on my feet!

At that exact instant I remembered Monica's sisterly remark, *Oh, let's have a Feel-Sorry-For-Darcy Day!* Just then, a wispy yellow butterfly fluttered right past my face. It frolicked in front of me as though he were introducing himself, ignoring the sweet smelling flowers by our driveway. My new friend lingered for a moment and then skipped on its way over our neighbor's fence. What timing!

There's no reason to feel sorry for myself, is there, God? I don't like other people feeling sorry for me; why should I feel that way?

The little yellow butterfly flipped back over the fence and danced across my path again, just as though God were sending a message: "You said it, Darcy!"

As fast as my sad feelings had come, they were gone. I smiled inside and out, as though some big super secret was now mine—I honestly felt as though God had spoken directly to me. I thought about that Bible verse, "I will never leave you nor forsake you. I am with you always, even until the end of the age."

The friendly butterfly danced around the foot pedals of my wheelchair. That's it, I decided. I promised myself that whenever I saw a butterfly, I would be reminded of God and His care for me. It would be a pact between God and me and the butterflies!

The wind whooshed, whisking the butterfly back over the fence. As I waved goodbye to my friend, I felt a brand new kind of . . . well, joy. Not just happy feelings, but the sort of joy in the Bible that our pastor is always talking about. I had never sensed it before like this. It was as if something bigger and grander than me was happening all around, and I wanted to be a part of it. It was like seeing the Grand Canyon or Niagara Falls for the first time. I can't explain it—maybe it was one of those grown-up feelings that you can't put into words when you're a kid.

This is who I really am, I thought with a smile. *Not the always-ready-with-a-joke kind of a kid that most of my friends at school know me as.*

After dinner I was dying to tell someone what I had learned that afternoon. I thought of calling Mandy or even April, thinking she might be back from Cincinnati. If I had the nerve, I would have called Chip. I even toyed with telling Monica. But I didn't tell anyone.

I snuggled up in bed and wrote to my Box.

5

Butterflies, butterflies everywhere! Yellow ones lighted on the bushes by the front door as I wheeled down the driveway. With a bump-bump I coasted into the street and along the curb, passing more butterflies on the clover that covered our neighbor's wooden fence. Wheeling around the bumpy sidewalk and down the long corridor of maple trees, I passed the old Siamese cat, who batted at another teasing butterfly from his perch on the picket fence. Our neighborhood seemed to be ablaze with butterflies.

And every time I saw one, I couldn't help

but break out into a big smile. What a neat way to remember Jesus. It was good to know that I really was a part of something—Someone—so much bigger than I am.

I was beginning to feel a lot more, well, mature. Maybe thinking and talking about God makes you feel that way. I'm not sure. All I knew was that I hadn't felt sorry for myself in weeks.

I had outgrown Rabbie after all—I didn't need a stuffed animal to help me talk to God—but I kept him wedged in the corner of my bedpost to watch me write letters to my Box. Actually, my letters were less like the pages of a diary and more like the notes Monica makes in the back of her Bible. In fact, I had occasionally borrowed Monica's Bible to copy some of her underlined verses.

Dear Box,
I've hardly had time to worry about junior high school, and almost no time to worry about family camp. To be honest, I'm kind of excited about camp, even though I won't be rooming with the rest of my friends. I can't wait to be in the mountains and under the stars and to smell the pine trees. Even God knows how I feel—I

*found this cool verse in my sister's Bible.
"When I consider your heavens ... the
moon and the stars which you have set in
place, what is man that you are mindful of
him?"*

*That's exactly how I feel. I haven't talked
to Mandy yet about all this. I haven't even
told her about the butterflies. It's all so
special, I want to keep it to myself for now.*
Darcy."

I stopped writing and leaned back with
my hands behind my head. Yep, things had
been different ever since that breezy day in
the driveway. It was great to be free of feeling sorry for myself. All those trapped, ugly
feelings were gone, now that I sensed God
was so much closer. Nothing could spoil
that.

I heard the phone ring down the hallway.
Mom yelled that it was for me. I threw my
Box on the bed and wheeled up the hall.

"Hello?"

"Hi, Darcy, it's April."

"April? I thought you were in Cincinnati."

"We got back a couple of days ago. It was
bo-o-ring. But now I'm back," she giggled.

"Oh. Great." Why did I have this funny
clutch in my throat?

44

"I'm just calling to tell you that I'm sorry you won't be rooming with us kids at family camp. I ran into Mandy and her mom at the mall yesterday, and she told me the bad news."

Bother! Why did Mandy have to open her mouth—especially to April!

I took a deep breath and scrambled for a cool-as-a-cucumber response. "No big deal. I'll be with you guys every step of the way." My old jokester tone of voice was back.

"Well, maybe so," said April. "But don't worry if things get too fast for you. I'll make sure the rest of the kids don't leave you in the dust." There she was with that snobby tone of voice again.

"Dust? Nothing kicks up dust like these wheels of mine when I get going," I laughed.

"Well . . . good. But those mountain trails are pretty steep, and nothing is really level there. But don't worry, we'll slow down for you. Soo-o-o, I'll see you at camp." April gurgled goodbye.

I put down the receiver and rubbed my throat to get rid of that clutching feeling. How could she ruin such a perfect day . . . such a perfect week? All my good feelings were suddenly down the drain.

I went back to my bedroom and sat. I threw my Box back in its drawer—I didn't feel like writing any more. I didn't even feel like praying.

Suddenly God felt very far away. It made me mad that my feelings about Him could change so drastically, and in only a matter of moments. For an instant I fumed over the idea that God was more involved with the heavens and the moon and the stars than He was with how I felt right now.

Yeah, God, that verse was right. Who am I, little old Darcy DeAngelis, that you should be mindful of me? Looking up, I caught my reflection in my dresser mirror and discovered that I looked as ugly as I felt.

Camp was going to be a lot harder than I thought.

6

Our overloaded station wagon rumbled up the dirt road leading to the camp and slid to a halt in a cloud of dust. Other families from church were just pulling in.

"Isn't it great to be back! Wow!" Monica whistled as she opened the trunk to get out my wheelchair. I peered out my side window at the dull gray cliffs which rose high behind the meadow grove of pine trees surrounding the lodge and cabins. On one side of the meadow was a glassy lake where canoes and motorboats were tied to the dock. On the other side, just beyond the rustic buildings, stood a barn and corral.

Behind it all were the towering distant mountains. We heard the echo of a group singing camp songs somewhere. I spied a chipmunk on a nearby rock and pointed him out to Josh. It was a beautiful place.

By the time Monica and Mom helped me into the chair, Dad had gotten our cabin assignments and was unloading suitcases, blankets, and pillows.

"Hi yah, Darce!" It was Amy, another friend from church. If she was around, the other kids couldn't be far behind. I wished Mandy were with me, but her folks had stopped for gas a ways back. They'd be along soon.

Mom piled two duffelbags on my lap, and I followed her to our cabin. It was built of logs with crusty red bark. A big spread of bleached white antlers hung over the screen door which, I noticed when Mom swung it open, needed a good squirt of WD-40. The wooden ramp worked fine.

I surveyed the scene from the porch. Across the gully stood the pre-teen cabin, a bigger one than ours with a hitching post in front. I recognized a couple of kids and waved. Further back in the trees stood Monica's high school cabin. Josh's Woodchuck lodge, I recalled, was down by the corral. I noticed Chipper and his buddy, Paul, heaving their sleeping bags and rolls up the path to their cabin. Almost everybody was here.

"Hi, your name's Darcy, isn't it?" asked a voice behind me. An older girl—maybe college age—in a white sweatshirt with a whistle 'round her neck lifted the duffel off my lap.

"My name is Betsy. I'm counseling the rest of the girls in the other cabin." She pointed over her shoulder with her thumb.

I smiled, brushed away my bangs, and shifted my weight in my wheelchair while she continued.

"If it's okay with your parents, how about joining the rest of the gang at our dinner table tonight?"

"Hey, that goes without saying," I said in an off-the-cuff way.

"Great, Darcy. We'll see you at six-thirty." She slapped my shoulder with her clipboard and headed back over the gully. I watched Betsy climb the other side and sighed. The trail didn't look fit for wheelchair use.

Monica and Josh were already off with their friends. Mom and Dad hobnobbed with some other parents. A horn honked down at the parking corral—Mandy was here! Camp had begun.

The pine-log dining hall/lodge was awesome. Buffalo heads and Indian blankets hang on the walls. There's even a big old bear skin hanging over the fireplace at the far end. Willowbrook, it isn't!

Mandy helped me through the cafeteria line, placing spaghetti and meat balls on the tray in my lap. My legs fit easily underneath the table, and we made sure we sat near Betsy.

It was clear she was fast becoming the kids' favorite, and no wonder—she treated all of us like regular people. April hogged the conversation, but I noticed that Betsy seemed really interested in all of us, asking about our favorite teachers and hobbies. We even got to vote on what we'd like to do first thing after breakfast the next morning.

A couple said volleyball and one voted for swimming, but most everybody wanted to go for a hike up the cliffs. All except me. I pasted on a smile, sat quietly, and kept my vote to myself.

We left the dining lodge and stopped on the patio to yawn and stretch. It was a cool and exciting evening, and the stars shone crystal-clear above us. I took a deep breath. The pine air was crisp and sweet, and I wished we were having a campfire tonight.

Mandy pushed me up the path toward the cabins while Betsy walked along, swinging her whistle. Ahead of us, Chip threw pebbles. His silhouette looked large in the dark. It felt good that he wanted to walk with us rather than Paul, Jared, or the other guys. Ahead of him, April skipped up the path.

"Are you guys all going on the hike?" she shouted back to us.

"You bet," shouted Chip. "Got my hiking boots ready."

A big "Shhh!" came from another counselor behind us.

Just like April to start trouble, I thought. *She probably wants me to shout back my answer so the whole camp will know that I can't go on the hike!*

April skipped up to us. "Are you going, Mandy?"

Mandy stopped pushing and rubbed her palms on her jeans. "I guess. Sure." I knew if we had been alone, she would have run the idea by me first.

"Boy, I really wish I could go, but—but

Monica is helping me get into the lake tomorrow."

"Well, I hope you have as much fun as we will." April hopscotched back up the path.

Chipper turned around. "Sometimes she can be a real jerk."

Betsy didn't crack a smile, but Mandy and I giggled.

When we reached the place where the path split toward the adult cabins, Chip waited for a moment. "We'll miss you on the hike. Have a good time with your sister, okay, Wheels?"

"Yeah, sure," I said.

I had no idea what Monica was planning after the morning meeting. I felt guilty—I had lied.

7

The next morning I scurried out of bed early, whipped a brush through my hair, and started out the cabin door. I had missed breakfast, but I wasn't going to miss the kids!

"Where *are* you rushing to, Darcy?" Mom said as she folded a blanket.

"To a hike ... uh, I mean, to go swimming."

"Honey, you don't have your bathing suit on."

I shot a glance down at my body. She was right. All I had on was my jeans and a T-shirt.

"Oops, I forgot." I whirled my chair around and grabbed my navy racing-back suit out of the suitcase. I looped it around the handle of my wheelchair in plain sight so everyone would *know* I was planning to swim.

"Darcy, what's going on?" demanded Mother. "You know you just can't change clothes down by the lake. You have to lie down on a—"

I was out the door, careening on one wheel as I held on to the cabin post. I took the long path over to the girls' cabin, where the group was beginning to gather. April, I noticed, had on brand new hiking boots with high tops and red laces—I might have known. Chip and Jared had canteens slung over their shoulders. Betsy walked up to me as she knotted a bandanna around her neck.

"I hope you have a good time at the lake, Darcy." She squeezed the nylon material of my swimsuit. "Nice suit," she offered and then looked me straight in the eyes.

I felt like she could see into my brain, guessing the truth as Mom or Mandy would. But I wasn't embarrassed, and I looked right back into her eyes. I knew that Betsy had found me out, but that she understood.

She didn't feel sorry for me; she just *felt* for me, and that was okay.

"Anything I can do for you before we go?" she asked.

I shrugged my shoulders and grinned.

"Hey, gang! Let's meet Darcy at the lake after the hike, okay?"

The kids cheered, grabbed their packs, and headed up the trail. I sat, twirling my swimsuit, and watched until the last person disappeared around the corner.

I wish I had my Box right now, I thought to myself. But since I had left it at home, I could only imagine what I would write. *If only I weren't so different. If only I could go on that hike. Splash my feet in a stream ... feel slippery pebbles with my toes ... vault over a fallen tree ... stomp in mud ... kick stones down the trail ... wonder at the view from on top of that mountain.* I shaded my eyes to see if I could spot my friends on the upper trail.

I felt tears coming. Another creepy old feel-sorry-for-Darcy day. *Nope, I'm not going to let it happen!* I decided. I glanced around for a butterfly, but the only moving thing was a nearby pine branch that rustled in the breeze.

"Please, dear God," I prayed, as I squished my fists against my eyes. "If ever I needed a butterfly, it's now. Please, if I can't go hiking and get out into Your wonderful creation—" I paused and thought. "Would You bring Your creation close to me? Bring by a butterfly, or a caterpillar. Anything!"

I sniffed and looked around again. I sat there for what felt like ten solid minutes. Nothing moved. Not even the pine branch.

I stuffed my swimsuit under my leg and slowly wheeled back to our cabin. Mom and Dad were heading out the door for a late-shift breakfast, and I followed them to the dining hall.

"No early swim?" Mom asked. She smoothed my hair as though she could tell I had been crying.

"No swim," I answered flatly.

We found some seats. Dad dug into a plate of hot pancakes and syrup, and Mom sipped coffee and nibbled on toast and jam. I wasn't hungry.

After we ate, I went down to the lake with Mom and Dad. Monica was there, too. We watched Josh trying his best to paddle a canoe straight. I tried to chip in with the rest of the family's cheers for Josh's efforts, but I couldn't get into the spirit of things. I kept wondering what the other kids were doing.

I looked around, thinking there might be a few butterflies flittering in the reeds by the shoreline. None.

Just then, I heard a lot of shouting and laughing back near the cabins. I glanced at my watch. It must be the gang back from the hike. "Go for it, Josh!" I yelled with sudden enthusiasm, and then I angled my chair up the path.

"What's the hurry?" Monica asked over her shoulder.

"The kids are expecting me!"

When I screeched to a stop at the pre-teen cabin, the guys were just throwing off their backpacks and collapsing on rocks, exhausted.

"How was it, everybody?"

A couple guys were comparing blisters while several of the girls untied their bandannas and wiped their faces and arms. I craned my neck and noticed April, who waved as she flung her arm around Amy. I half-heartedly waved back.

"Where's Mandy?" I called.

April thumbed in the direction of Betsy,

who was pouring out her canteen in the dirt. Beside her sat Mandy—and Chipper, talking intently.

"Hey, Chipmunk!" Jared called to Chip, and everybody broke up.

"Chipmunk?" I said, as I wheeled up to Mandy. She had been cutting up, but she put on a straight face as soon as she saw me. Ouch.

"Chip Chipmunk," April yelled. "What a name to haunt you all the way into junior high!"

Mandy stood up and dusted off her jeans. She explained that Chipper's backpack had been raided by a family of chipmunks who stole every one of his cookies. Everyone cracked up again as she retold the story. Chip just sat there cool and collected with barely a blush. Betsy smiled, too. I struggled hard not to feel left out.

As the kids got up and drifted toward the cabins, Chip stood and snapped his bandanna at my wheels. "Did you find a baby-sitter?" he said in a good-natured way. I've laughed a dozen times at silly digs like that. But this time his joke—even though he didn't mean it—was too close for comfort.

"You really missed it at the lake," I said.

"What went on?" Mandy asked, as the three of us fell in line behind Betsy.

"Oh, just some fantastic canoeing and stuff," I said, giving the impression that I was the one who had been in the canoe.

I suddenly felt sick to my stomach. I couldn't tell if it was because I hadn't eaten or because I was trying ridiculously hard to impress my friends. I felt like everybody knew that I was faking. When the path split, I wheeled toward my cabin, saying I need money for the snack bar. Mandy and Chipper walked on, but Betsy hesitated.

I didn't dare look back at her—I could feel my face getting hot. Where, oh where, were my butterflies?!

As I bumped over the doorsill, I sensed Betsy enter the cabin behind me.

"Need some help looking for change?" she asked.

I couldn't believe it. I would have to go through with this dumb charade. "Sure. My purse is over on the bunk."

Betsy tossed it on my lap. "Are you okay?"

"Of course I am," I said, hiding my face as I rummaged through my purse.

There was a long silence and I felt her

standing there, unmoving.

"Really?" Betsy asked as she knelt by my chair.

I took one look into her eyes and burst into tears. I blubbered something about hating feeling different and wishing I had my legs and wanting to go hiking and swimming and even walking with Chip and Mandy. And that was another thing—I hated feeling jealous over the time Chip and Mandy were spending together. Chip and Mandy! Two of my best friends!

"Oh, Darcy," Betsy said as she pulled me to her. "It's hard being different, isn't it?"

I nodded. It felt good to rest my head against her.

"But you've got so much going for you. And I'm not talking only about your great mop of hair, and blue eyes and freckles." She pushed my nose with her finger. "You care about the feelings of others . . . and you feel things deeply . . . and you handle some pretty tough situations, young lady, a lot better than many adults would. A lot better than I would."

"That still doesn't help these feelings."

"God knows, Darcy. He cares, about those who can't do things like everyone else."

"I prayed about that today," I said, sniffing. "Since I couldn't go on the hike, I asked God to bring His creation close to me—but nothing happened. At least you guys got close up to a chipmunk. Not even a caterpillar came near me."

"God didn't answer your prayer?" Betsy brushed my wet hair off my face.

I shook my head no.

"Maybe . . . maybe He's waiting."

"What for?"

"Oh, maybe to give you an answer you never dreamed of. Something very special." Betsy smiled a great big smile and held me at arm's length. "Something very different."

8

The next few days were a whirlwind! The camp schedule kept me so busy that I almost forgot about the disastrous morning of the hike.

Josh was picked to paddle on a canoe team. Monica invited Mandy and me to scrimmage with her volleyball friends. There was a potato sack race and a contest for eating watermelon. In between time, I hung around with kids my age, inner tubing in the lake or kicking around the coral. And, of course, there were the morning and evening meetings with our pastor and the rest of the church family.

For the past few evenings, Pastor Rob had been talking about prayer. Fortunately he kept his messages short—all of us were zonked from playing in the lake and racing around in the hot sun. But this evening, I didn't dare nod off. Something he said got my attention.

Pastor Rob stood up front with one hand in his pocket and the other hand holding his open Bible. He said that God always answers prayer. Sometimes it's a yes answer and sometimes it's no. And then there are other kinds. God may wait a long time before He gets back to us with His reply. Then again, He may answer quickly, but in a far different way than we ever expected.

I sat, picking the day's dirt from underneath my fingernails but listening intently. I had forgotten all about the prayer I had prayed the morning of the hike, asking God to bring His creation close to me. I wondered if God had forgotten about it, too. Probably He had brushed off my request as too silly or small to take notice of. Maybe that was my answer—God was telling me I should shape up and get serious, when it came to praying. I should pray only about important stuff.

Pastor Rob closed his Bible and prayed and told us all good night. I pulled on my sweatshirt and wheeled behind Mom and Dad as we strolled slowly back to our cabin, enjoying the quilt of stars above.

It was the most star-filled sky I had ever seen. So many stars, it was scary. *"When I consider the heavens and moon and the stars ..."* I remembered the verse I had read in Monica's Bible weeks ago. *With all of your great big universe, God, I don't know how you have time to think about me. Maybe it would help if I kept my prayers more serious ... more realistic ... only brought You the big and important stuff.*

Having said that, I felt sad. As though I had given up or something.

Back at our cabin, Monica was stacking wood and kindling in the fire pit. Tonight our family was going to roast marshmallows and eat s'mores. My parents also said it was okay for Mandy to join us.

As the fire began to crackle and blaze, we spread blankets over the logs around the pit, parking ourselves away from the smoke. Monica whittled our sticks to a sharp point, while Mandy and I ripped open the plastic bags of marshmallows.

I speared a marshmallow in the exact middle and pushed it up the stick. Monica was already pulling a hot gooey one off her stick. I was glad that she wanted to spend some time with us tonight.

The glow of hot coals felt good on my face. I could hear crickets chirping in the gully and Mom humming inside the cabin. It was a special night.

As Monica speared another marshmallow, something moved behind her shoulder, catching my eye. I strained to see in the dark. There was something large and black moving slowly behind her. I put down my stick and rubbed the smoke from my eyes. It was a big, black dog.

Monica held her marshmallow over the fire and began singing the same tune that had floated out from Mom's cabin.

The giant dog stopped right behind Monica and rose slowly to its back feet. *Dogs don't do that*, I thought, and then I realized that it wasn't a dog. It was a bear! And it was only inches from my sister.

"Monica, don't move!" I whispered hoarsely.

My sister gave me one of her queer looks.

Mandy stopped rummaging through the bag of marshmallows.

"Monica, there's a bear right behind you!"

"Da-a-a-rcy," Monica groaned. "Would you quit with your dumb jokes."

Mandy shielded her eyes to see if there was anything there.

The bear bobbed his head, sniffing chocolate and graham crackers and marshmallows. Suddenly he rose higher.

"Monica, listen to me! There'a a bear —and he's right there!" I directed behind her with my eyes.

I could tell she realized now it was no joke. She calmly put down her stick, stood up, turned, and came within inches of a shiny black wet nose!

"Oh my—" she stifled a scream and sat back down, tightly grasping the log. "There's a bear right behind me," she whispered, without moving a muscle.

"Don't move. Don't move!" I hushed her.

Mandy dropped everything and crouched next to my wheelchair. "What'll we do?!"

The bear sniffed Monica's sweater, sniffed down the side of her leg, and then licked some burnt marshmallows in the dirt. Now that he was out in front of the fire, we saw

66

what a giant of a bear he was. His black coat shone in the firelight, and his claws were long and curled. As he chewed the sticky marshmallows, we could see his long pink tongue and gleaming sharp teeth. He slurped and grunted for more.

When he began to move toward me, Monica sprawled backward off her log.

Mandy clutched the side of my wheelchair tighter. "What should we do?" She was near panic.

"Sit still!" I whispered. "He just wants marshmallows . . . I hope."

The huge bear lumbered around the fire pit and began sniffing the foot pedals of my wheelchair. He snorted as he nosed the blanket which covered my legs. I slid my hands between my legs, afraid he might smell chocolate and marshmallow on my fingers. I couldn't believe it—a bear, practically in my lap! I was frozen with excitement. I sat more still than I ever had in my paralyzed life!

When the bear meandered around the back of my chair, Mandy bolted. She stumbled over a few rocks to get out of the bear's way, and dashed toward Monica, who was hiding behind a tree.

There I sat, helpless and alone with a giant bear. I couldn't get away even if I wanted to—the front wheels of my chair were wedged tightly between two rocks.

Just then I realized my hands were squeezing a couple of squished marshmallows between my knees, and I had a bright idea.

"Here, Mr. Bear," I coaxed, as I tossed the treats away from the fire pit. "Go get them!"

His big head turned. He sniffed and followed the marshmallows as they bounced on the dirt.

Just then my mother threw open the cabin door. "What's going on out there?" she called.

That was enough to scare the bear. He howled and lunged past the fire, overturning pots and pans, and disappeared into the darkness.

A jumble of shouting and scurrying followed. My folks yelled to our neighbors' cabins. Screen doors slammed, flashlight beams crisscrossed the woods, and somebody blew a whistle somewhere. The whole camp was in an uproar over the bear.

"Mrs. DeAngelis, are you all right?" I heard Betsy ask Mom.

"Tell us what happened!" I heard Chipper's voice as he scrambled up the gully.

"Darcy saw everything. She was great!" Mandy cheered.

Suddenly everyone was crowded around the fire pit with their eyes on me. "I ... I guess it was good that I couldn't move. He didn't bother me at all," I brightened.

"Weren't you *scared?*" April asked, wide-eyed.

I thought for a moment. No, I told them, I wasn't. I was thrilled! To think that I got that close to a real bear! Now that the panic had settled, we all treated the ruckus as an adventure.

"What a brilliant idea—tossing those marshmallows to get the bear away from us," Monica said. "I had a whole bagful, and all I could think of was hiding them from him!"

"Yes, and a lot of help you and Mandy were," my mother chided. "Leaving Darcy to fend for herself."

"I knew he wouldn't hurt me, Mom. That's one good thing about this wheel-chair—I sat really still."

"Yep, that's one thing you do better than anybody. Sit still!" Monica laughed.

"What did the bear look like, Darce?" asked Chipper.

After the story was re-hashed several times, the crowd began to break up and return to their cabins. Betsy walked up behind and crossed her arms around me. She hugged me hard and pressed her cheek against mine.

"Well?" she asked.

"Well, what?"

"Well, what do you think about this for a first-class answer to your prayer?"

I was stunned. "You're absolutely right," I marveled. "Man, that was no chipmunk or caterpillar. Wow! God brought me a bear."

"It's like God saying something special, something different just for you," Betsy whispered.

After Mom helped me to bed, I lay there watching the moonlight pour through the window. I was too excited to sleep, but not only about my bear. I kept replaying what Betsy had said. *God was saying something special, something different just for me.*

No prayer was too small or silly to talk to God about. And what Pastor Rob had said was true—God may wait to give us an entirely different answer from what we expect.

And something else hit me, too. If God is concerned enough to listen to a stupid little prayer like "bring your creation close to me," then how much more will He care about big and important prayers? Like prayers about my wheelchair ... or splashing my feet in a stream ... or even junior high school?

God, you did something different tonight. You did more than I expected. Maybe being different isn't all that bad. But can I really be different and like it? Honestly? I don't know if I can. Show me how, please.

As a cloud passed over the moon, I realized what I had prayed. I had no idea how God would answer. But I knew He would—and I guessed it would be very unusual!

9

Breakfast with the family was a blast the next morning. I was hungry, for a change, and had no trouble devouring waffles, bacon and eggs, and fried potatoes and ketchup. It wasn't easy answering with my mouth full every time somebody came up and asked Monica and me about our bear.

"Ready for the volleyball match, Darcy?" asked Mandy as she trotted up to our table, bouncing a ball.

"Yeow, I almost forgot," I said, wiping my mouth and crumpling my napkin. "And here I just pigged out. Have you guys picked teams, yet?"

"Well, sort of. At least we picked captains."

"Who?" I said as I unlocked my brakes and pushed myself back from the table.

"Chip's Chipmunks is one team," Mandy said, twirling the ball on her finger. "And the other is Darcy's Bears!"

"You're kidding."

"Nope, I'm not. Isn't that super?" She grinned. "We got together and voted before breakfast."

"Darcy, isn't that nice," Mom said as she took a last sip of her coffee.

"Will you guys come and watch?" I asked the family. Josh squirmed, and I shook a playful fist at him. "Josh, you'd better. I watched you in that canoe."

Dad gave him a look that said, "She's right."

"All right, all right," Josh gave in.

A few minutes later Mandy and I were down by the volleyball court. It wasn't much of a court, but at least the net was high and taut with only a few holes. The dirt was hard—good for me to wheel on, but not so good for everyone else to fall on.

I flipped the ball in my hands, making certain it was pumped up enough. Betsy was at the other end of the court sifting white powder on the end line. Kids began to gather from the cabins and dining hall when Betsy blew her whistle.

It was time for the game to begin.

"Okay, Chip? Darcy?" Betsy pointed at us. "Begin your picks."

The count off went quickly. Chipper tried to hog all the best guys, but at least I got Paul, who everybody said was great at the net. Amy went over to the other side. Finally we were down to Rosita, a new kid at church, and April, who everybody knew was great with hair gel and pearl combs, but not much good with a dirty, sweaty volleyball.

I felt bad that they were left last. I knew how it felt.

"April, you're with us," I called.

"Thanks for nothing," she snorted as she brushed past me.

"Heads up!" Betsy called. "Darcy, your team will serve first, rotating around you. Got it?"

"Okay, Bears, let's get it together!" I yelled.

Mom, Dad, Monica, and Josh cheered from the sidelines, along with a bunch of other families.

We made five points on our first service and gave the ball over to Chip who returned the serve for the Chipmunks. After two points were scored, the serve was ours again, and April rotated around as our next server. She gave a giant swing, and the ball barely skimmed the net, dropping dead on the Chipmunks' side.

"Good going!" I yelled. April looked like she needed cheering up.

Unfortunately, her next serve didn't make it across the net, and the Chipmunks rallied, gaining on us by three points. Our team rotated again. April shifted into the position next to my wheelchair.

I can't remember exactly what happened next. All I can say is the ball sailed our way, I called for it, and April lunged in front of me. I felt a clunk, and my wheelchair nearly tipped over onto April who was sprawled on the hard dirt.

"Ooow! I broke it . . . I broke it!" April cried. She looked terrible.

Betsy blew her whistle and called the kids to her side as some parents came running. I sat there, shocked and stunned. What had I done?

April sobbed as Dad leaned over her and

asked where it hurt. She pointed at her ankle. It already looked swollen.

"That dumb wheelchair! I wouldn't have fallen if it weren't in the way!"

I felt awful. I didn't say anything. I couldn't.

"Not that it was *your* fault, Darcy," April said between sniffs. "It was just that stupid chair."

That stupid chair was a part of me, whether April realized it or not. Somehow I couldn't help but think she knew that. I gripped my wheels and began to back my chair away.

"Don't move!" April whined. "You'll probably run over my other foot."

"I didn't touch you, April . . . you tripped over me, remember?"

Dad glared. "That'll be enough, Darcy!"

"But, Dad—"

"No buts!"

"It really hurts, Mr. DeAngelis," April piled it on.

By that time April's parents had arrived on the scene. Together with my father, they carried April to the first aid post like a bunch of paramedics.

I knew I hadn't done anything wrong, but

that didn't make me feel any better. My wheelchair and I seemed to be in the middle of another big scene.

After sending the other kids away from the court, Betsy came and put her arm around me. "I saw you almost fall out of that chair. Are you okay?"

I nodded, a little dejected.

"Don't take it hard," Betsy said, rubbing my shoulder. "I think April will be okay. I'm going to go see to her now."

Betsy started to walk away, and then she paused and turned to say, "Everything will work out okay, Darcy. You'll see."

Just as I was about to sink back into the blues, I noticed two butterflies flitting around the other side of the empty volleyball court. They danced and pranced and then went on their way. It was all the reminder I needed.

After all, this wasn't a federal emergency. Nobody had dropped a bomb, and the National Guard had not been called out. April would live. I wouldn't die. Life would go on.

So, I wasn't going to feel sorry for myself, or for April either. Somehow, this would all work out, just as Betsy said. Having thought all this through, I congratulated myself on my very mature thinking.

Then Monica walked up. "Boy, are you in the doghouse," she said.

I watched Betsy walk through the door of the first-aid post. "Maybe," I answered. "Then again, maybe not."

10

When I wheeled into the dining lodge for lunch, I spotted April with her foot up on the bench and a pair of crutches leaning against the totem pole behind her. She had sprained her ankle, and the camp nurse told her to keep off of it as much as possible. That was going to drive April up the wall—she couldn't stand not being in the middle of the action.

I wheeled over to her family's table. "How are you feeling?"

Her mother and dad nodded and smiled, but by the way they acted I suspected that April had made it all sound like my fault.

April fiddled with her fork. "Okay, I guess."

"I'm really sorry about the accident." I made an honest attempt to apologize.

April leaned on her elbow and stared at her plate. Her mother chimed in, "I guess we all have to realize that you can't move that wheelchair of yours out of the way very quickly."

I felt my anger rising, and I wanted to explain that I had called for the ball, and it was April who made the wrong move. But I didn't. "We all have our handicaps," I said, smiling. "And as I said, I'm really sorry."

April softened with my apology. "Well, it isn't hurting as bad as it was. I'm just sorry I'm going to miss out on Western Night."

Tonight all the cabins were supposed to dress up in wild west clothes for dinner. Pastor Rob was going to judge our getups and award prizes for the most unusual. I hadn't given it much thought.

"Well, I guess you and I will hang out together—'crips corner' and all that," I kidded.

From the look April shot back at me I could tell that she didn't appreciate my joke. Or maybe the truth hurt her, too—that it's hard being different from everyone else. Or, worse yet, maybe she couldn't stand the thought of having everyone thing of her as handicapped—like me.

I said goodbye and wheeled over to Betsy, who was finishing up lunch with the rest of the kids. Everyone was jabbering about what to wear for Western Night. Jared wanted to be a cowboy. A couple of guys wanted to be snake-oil salesmen, Amy wanted to be Annie Oakley, and Chipper and his friends thought it would be a good idea to be a sheriff and his posse.

I noticed as I quietly ate my dinner that Rosita, the Hispanic girl, had nothing to say. Like me, she sat and listened as the ideas flew back and forth.

Betsy pushed back her tray and stood up. "Listen, gang, all your suggestions sound terrific. But remember that we have to come up with one theme for our entire cabin. Everybody's got to play a part, okay?"

"But that's impossible," Chip insisted.

"I don't think so," Betsy answered. "Besides, this will help you to think as a team."

A couple of the kids groaned as they stood

and took back their trays. After a few minutes, the only ones left were Betsy, Rosita, Mandy, and me.

"Well, girls, any ideas?" Betsy leaned on her elbows.

"I like the posse idea," Mandy said. "At least most everybody could join in."

" 'Most everybody' isn't the entire group. We need to include everyone," Betsy said. She eyed Rosita, who had just left to return her tray. "And remember April, too."

"What about April?" I asked.

"She thinks she has to miss out on tonight because of her sprained ankle," Betsy explained.

"Sprained ankle? Big deal," said Mandy. "Darcy's whole body is one big sprain, and she's not going to let herself miss out. Right, Darce?"

Betsy continued, "That's all the more reason, Darcy, for you to reach out to April. Help her understand how to cope."

"Me, help April? She'd throw up at the idea of saying her name and the word 'handicap' in the same sentence. She doesn't want my help."

"Listen, you two. You are bright, caring, and very special kids. And right now your friend April needs you. She's feeling insecure," Betsy said.

"Insecure? Not Miss Center-of-Attention," Mandy laughed.

I agreed with Mandy. April seemed anything but insecure. And even if she was feeling down on herself, what was the big deal about a sprained ankle? I struggled hard not to compare my own paralysis with her little sprain. If anybody had a right to feel insecure, it was me.

I glanced over my shoulder at April, who was tucking a crutch under each shoulder. I knew I was being a snob.

"So, as I was saying . . . any better ideas?" Betsy asked again.

I leaned my head on my fists, thinking hard. We needed something different. Something very special. And it had to include everybody. Slowly a light began to dawn. I looked at Mandy, who gave me a big grin in return.

"Uh oh. What are you two up to?" Betsy asked.

"I'm not sure," Mandy said with a laugh. "But I know that look. Darcy just had a brilliant idea!"

It was brilliant—or at least terrific. I

threw my napkin on the table, whipped my wheelchair around, and headed for the dining lodge door. Mandy was only a step behind me.

"If you need any help, just holler," Betsy called, as we disappeared out the door.

11

"Sheets?"

"Check," said Mandy.

"Fifteen yards of clothesline?"

"Check."

"Five coat hangers? Cardboard? Paint and brush? And, let's see, a riding crop swiped off the tack room wall?"

"Check . . . check . . . check. Everything's here."

My parents' cabin floor was strewn with coat hangers and yards of clothesline and baling twine.

"You think this is going to work?" Mandy asked, as she pulled and twisted the wire.

"Sure I do," I answered. "But this—" I gestured toward the mess, "is the easy part. The hard part will be—"

"Convincing the others!" finished Mandy.

"Yeah. Especially April."

Mandy seemed to be absorbed in her work. "April. Hmmm. Do you really think she's 'insecure,' the way Betsy said?"

How should I know? I thought. I'm just a kid myself, not a shrink. April generally got louder every time the spotlight shifted away from her. That was April. But to choose to eat with her parents rather than all her friends? To bow out of Western Night with not so much as a whimper? *That* was a different April.

I sighed and said, "I know how hard it is to be different. As Dad is always saying, 'We all have handicaps.' It sure doesn't help when people don't include you ... don't reach out to you."

"Am I hearing right? Can this be Darcy the joker, who doesn't seem to give two hoots that her wheelchair makes her different?" Mandy looked straight at me.

I sighed again—a bigger sigh. Dear Mandy. I really hadn't been much of a friend to her lately. And now, sitting alone with her in this cozy cabin, surrounded by big trees and an even bigger sky, I decided it was time to bring her up-to-date.

"I'm tired of telling jokes, Mandy. There's a lot of stuff going on inside of me. Things I haven't told you about." I told her about the day we graduated from elementary school and my fright about junior high. I told her about my Box and my loneliness, especially here at camp in the beginning. And I told her about my butterflies, and how much closer I've drawn to God.

"And you told all this stuff to a . . . a box? and a toy rabbit? Not to me, your best friend?" Mandy looked a little hurt.

"I was afraid. Especially since you and Chip seemed to have gotten so thick."

"Thick? Yuck!" Mandy gagged. "Well, maybe not 'yuck,' but close. Darcy, this is your friend speaking. And I'm telling you straight that Chipper has definite eyes for you, not me."

I was shocked. "Me? What are you talking about?"

"Remember that day you wheeled up to us after our hike?"

I nodded. That was the time I saw the two of them resting on a log, whispering about things they didn't seem to want anyone else to hear. "The two of you looked pretty buddy-buddy."

Mandy rolled her eyes. "We were talking about you, dummy. He nearly died when you showed up. He was just asking me if he should have forgotten the hike and offered to stay behind to keep you company. Not that he felt sorry for you—he just wanted to be a friend."

I was hot with embarrassment, but I was dying to know more. "But ... but that stupid remark about baby-sitting?"

"Just a joke, Darce. No better, no worse than the silly jokes I've heard you say."

Mandy unwound a long story about how Chip wanted to help me but didn't know how. Did I want people to push me, or would I rather push myself? Should he offer to carry my books, or would that hurt my feelings? Should he walk beside me, push from behind, keep in front of me? He just didn't know.

The whole time I was listening to her, I kept thinking back on times I had noticed Chip. I had to admit my secret feelings for him. While he had grown taller and more handsome, he was still a regular buddy.

That's what drew me to him, and probably that's why I had grown jealous of Mandy without even realizing it.

"And remember last month at school when your wheelchair got a flat tire?" continued Mandy.

I nodded, a little confused.

"Chipper could have fixed it easily. But no, you insisted on having your dad come to school with his tire jack, when all the time Chip had a patch kit in the bike bag of his ten-speed. He was just too shy to say anything."

"Chipper, shy? April, insecure? The world's upside down. I guess Dad is right —everybody *does* have a handicap."

"Yeah, but you're miles ahead of most kids. You've got a lot of confidence. And you care about God . . . and others."

"Others!" I gasped and looked at my watch. "Mandy, Western Night is just a couple hours away, and we haven't even sold our plan to the others!"

We scrambled, gathering the sheets, rope, and wire into a bundle and slamming out the screen door. The afternoon light was fading as we hurried down the path toward the pre-teen cabins.

Betsy met us on the path. "Where have you guys been?" she said, throwing up her hands in mock panic. "I told the kids that you had a super idea—and at this point, it had *better* be super. We have to be at the dining hall in an hour and a half!"

"Okay, everybody!" I shouted. "Let me tell you our idea."

As the kids pressed around my wheelchair, I was kind of glad that we didn't have much time; that way nobody would put up a stink if they didn't quite go for my plan. But I had a feeling it would work out great. We put our heads together, and Mandy and I explained each kid's part.

After a moment or two, Jared straightened up and scratched his head. "I don't know about this," he muttered.

"Yeah. I don't know if I want to get down on my hands and knees," Paul grumbled.

A couple of the girls started to whine, too, but then Chip spoke up. "I think it's a great idea. It's original, and it includes everyone. Count me in!"

Whew. Mandy and I gave each other a look of relief. After Chip stood up for me, the rest of the guys fell in line. But I was most surprised at April's response.

"Darcy, I'm honored that you picked me for such a . . . a prominent role." She smiled sweetly. "Are you sure you want me to be the head person?"

"April, old buddy, I wouldn't have it any other way," I said, slapping her on the back.

A couple kids started painting the cardboard, and within minutes, it looked like the sides of an old covered wagon. Other kids began tearing sheets, rubbing them around in the dirt to make them look old and worn. Paul and Jared began twisting the big wire loops onto my wheelchair.

Mandy showed the other girls how to pull their hair up in two ponytails, high on top of their heads. Since Rosita's hair was so short, she had a little trouble getting her ponytails high enough on her head, so Amy helped her.

Jared and Paul looped the clothesline bridles over each of the girl's heads, laughing and pointing at their funny-looking ponytails.

Chip smeared ashes from the fire pit on April's cheeks and chin.

April winced. "Ugggh! Do I have to have that icky junk on my face?"

"Afraid so," Chip said as he wiped the

ashes off his hands. "You've got to look authentic—rough beard, bandanna, the whole bit." For the finishing touch he shoved on her head an old cowboy hat he had picked up at the corral. With the riding crop stuck in her hand for a whip, she looked perfect.

Jared and Paul threw the dirtied sheets over the wire loops, knotting them to the armrests of my wheelchair. My bright purple chair and I were slowly becoming obscured.

The kids scurried around, grabbing the items they needed for their parts in our cabin costume.

"Okay, is everybody ready?" Betsy waved us down the trail toward the dining hall.

We screeched to a stop at the door. We were late. Everyone else was already there, and my dad was just coming out the door to look for us.

"Where have you all been?" he said. "Everybody's waiting." He paused, apparently surveying our get-up. "Where's Darcy?"

"Hey, Dad, I'm in here!" I shouted from beneath sheets, wire, cardboard, and April, who was sitting on my lap.

The kids took up their positions, and Betsy made sure that everything and everyone was in place. Then she and Dad threw open the dining hall doors, and in we went.

Our two lead horses were Mandy and Amy, ambling along on their hands and knees, swaying and swinging in harness. The clothesline bridle linked them to the next pair of horses directly behind—Rosita and another girl, Jessie, who shook their heads and made their ponytails fly like a horse's mane. The clothesline harness continued, linking two other sets of girls who whinnied and snorted and kicked at their traces.

They pulled my wheelchair, which had been transformed into a Conestoga wagon. Jared and Paul had done a great job—they had secured the clothesline harness to my footpedals, and the sheets and painted cardboard made my chair look just like an old covered wagon.

April sat on my lap, reins and whip in hand. She took off the cowboy hat and waved as everyone cheered us through the dining hall.

Chipper and Jared brought up the rear as a cowboy riding his horse. The two of them were driving herd over a small group of cattle—the rest of the boys, who shuffled along on their hands and knees, mooing loud enough to raise the roof. Some of the "cattle" had even sneaked a few horns off the walls around camp and tied them around their heads with bandannas.

We circled the hall, April shouting and cracking her whip to her team. Chip, sitting atop Jared, yelled "Get along, little dawgies" and giving his horse an occasional kick in the side. We lumbered to a stop in front of the fireplace, where Pastor Rob stood at a microphone.

He laughed and shook his head at us. When he collected himself, he said, "I think we all agree that Western Night is a big success. We've been visited by the Pony Express, a group of Indian braves, and quite an assortment of cowboys and girls. But first prize goes to the preteens with their covered wagon theme. Tell me, wagon driver," he said leaning over to April with his microphone, "how do you keep all these horses in line?"

"See this?" April said, shaking her whip at him.

All the parents burst into laughter. Good

old April—yes, she certainly did belong in the junior high drama club.

Then the kids untangled themselves from the clothesline and stood and cheered. April couldn't get down until someone brought her the crutches. She slowly inched off my lap, tucked each crutch under her arm, and, to my surprise, turned around to give me a big hug.

"Oh, no." She giggled and pointed at my face.

I swiped my hand over my cheek. I had black junk all over me, too. But I didn't care. I was thrilled that we won. And even more, I was thrilled that we had really been a team—even April with her sprained ankle.

Betsy came up, reached inside my covered wagon, and gave me a another hug. "How did you dream up such a fantastic idea?"

"Isn't it great?" I glanced at the wire and sheets above me.

"Let's get you out of this contraption so you can have dinner. The rest of your team is waiting."

"Way to go, guys!" I congratulated everybody as I wheeled up to the table and found a place between Mandy and Chip. We were all too excited to eat.

Amy jabbered a mile a minute with Rosita. Even April seemed to forget about her sprained ankle.

Sitting there with my friends, I no longer felt bad. Oh, I was still different, but I was beginning to learn not to hate it. Being different meant being special . . . thinking of fun and crazy ways to do things, to include everyone. My dad really was right—every kid around that table had one kind of a handicap or another. Mine was just a little more obvious. But that, I decided, wasn't necessarily so bad.

12

The next day, family camp began to wind down. A few of the families left after breakfast, since there was no morning meeting scheduled. I had said goodbye to Betsy earlier, when she gave me a camp sticker for my wheelchair. Now I sat by our fire pit, thinking of how much I would miss camp and how I wished it didn't have to end so soon.

"Ready to head back to Willowbrook?" Mandy said as she walked up behind me from across the gully. Her blonde pigtails were tucked up under a bandanna, and she had a knapsack on her shoulders. I bet she would miss camp as much as I would.

"I guess so." I sighed, thinking about how different Willowbrook would look from this place. "I wonder how our friends the bulldog and that silly Siamese cat are doing."

Mandy plopped down beside me on a rock. "We won't be seeing them much when we get back. Our bus stop for junior high is down at the other end of the street."

It seemed years ago that we had walked down the road behind Willowbrook Elementary on our last day of school. For a few moments, Mandy and I sat in silence, basking in the warm morning sunlight on our shoulders. A hawk called out in the distance, and we heard his echo against the cliffs behind us. The wind stirred the pine trees, and we watched the breeze roll a little pinecone down the path. This had turned out to be a wonderful summer after all. Looking around me, I decided that this moment would be another one of those crystal-clear memories that I would keep forever.

"Hey, I like the way you handled April last night. That was a brilliant stroke of genius—having her sit on your lap as the lead player."

"How's she doing this morning?"

"I saw her hobbling out of the dining hall a few minutes ago. I think she and her parents are heading back soon."

I thought about April. She would probably miss camp, too, though no doubt she was dying to get out of her dirty clothes and into a hot shower.

"Remember what you asked me the other day about April? about her being insecure?"

"Yeah," Mandy said. "Have you decided she is?"

"Yes, I have. But I also think I'm pretty insecure . . . and so is Chip . . . and so are you, if you'll admit it."

Mandy picked up a stick we had used for marshmallows and scratched a design in the dirt. "You'll get no argument from me," she said. "Kids are supposed to be unsure of themselves . . . feel group pressure. Adults are always saying that we kids will do anything to be liked. I don't think I'd do *anything* to be liked, but I have to admit I've done a *few* things to be noticed before."

I gave her a funny look.

"Okay. You were honest with me the other day, now I'll be up front with you. There are times—not *all* the time—but some times when I've pushed you in your wheelchair so that kids would ... well, notice me."

"You're kidding, right?"

"No, I'm not," she said with surprising seriousness.

I began to giggle.

"I don't see what's so funny!"

That made me giggle harder.

"Quit *laughing*, you jerk," she said.

Before we knew it, we were both splitting our sides. I finally got control of myself and pointed at her. "So Mandy has a handicap, too."

"C'mon, I wouldn't call wanting to be noticed an actual handicap!"

"Well, something you don't like, anyway. Right?"

Mandy agreed.

I turned my wheelchair toward her. "Well, you know what? I discovered this week that there's something we can do about it. Remember the bear the other night?"

"Of course I remember the bear."

"Well, believe it or not, I don't think he came up on us by accident. That bear was an answer to prayer. But a pretty different answer than I ever expected."

Mandy gave me a funny look, not sure of where I was going.

I explained about my prayer about enjoying God's creation. "And last night. Dressing up like a covered wagon was no stroke of genius—it was another answer to prayer. I just decided to take all the things that I'm most insecure about—my paralyzed legs, my wheelchair, everything—and quit fighting them. Admit the things about me I don't like and quit trying to cover them up with jokes. Let God show me how to be different and really enjoy it. Does that make any sense?"

Mandy leaned on her elbows and nodded.

"I asked God to do something different in my life. Good grief, if He could bring a bear my way, then I figured coming up with an idea for Western Night wasn't too big an order."

"Yeah, well, I don't get big answers to prayers about bears and covered wagons." Mandy thought for a moment. "Then again, I guess I only pray when I'm bored. Bored in church or with homework, or bored when I don't have anything to do on a Friday night."

"That's what I'm telling you—I've learned

101

to pray and expect God to answer. Okay, sometimes the answer might be no. But then again, sometimes it's yes. And maybe a very different and unusual yes."

"It sounds like you've been listening to Pastor Rob's talks," Mandy said.

"Well, not *all* of his talks," I admitted, "but some."

A horn honked down at the parking corral. Mandy's folks were ready to leave. She stood and kicked dust from the fire pit off her hiking shoes.

"Well, I'm glad you've learned a lot about prayer," Mandy said, giving my shoulders a squeeze. "I think we're all going to need it next week, when we become full-fledged seventh graders. Jordan Junior High isn't going to be a picnic."

She jogged down the path to the car, stopping to turn and wave goodbye.

13

Dear Box,

I wish I could put into words how I feel right now. Camp was so neat. I've decided that I'm a real outdoors person. Maybe instead of being a social worker with kids, I should be a forest ranger (if they make fire towers accessible).

Being out in the mountains made me think a lot more about God. And then there was that awesome bear. And most of the time, a butterfly or two around.

I think I am finally learning to reach out to other people instead of feeling sorry for myself. Of course the big test is coming up to-

*morrow when I start junior high. I'm scared.
I know there will be a ton of problems, even
though Mom and Dad have talked to the
principal about my wheelchair.*

*I wrote on the inside of my notebook
(where no one else can see) a reminder. Jesus
said that He would always be with me, never
leave me and never forsake me. I hope He's
ready to go to school tomorrow.*

Your frightened friend, Darcy.

I folded my note, slipped it underneath
the rubberband with the others, and got
ready for bed. I had decided to wear my best
faded jeans with the pleats tomorrow and
my pink sweater with the lace collar. My
hair, which had really grown long since
June, could now be pulled back into a pearl
clasp to make a big, fluffy ponytail. I
couldn't decide between the little gold ear-
rings or the plastic hearts, but I knew for
sure I would wear the necklace Monica gave
me for my last birthday.

I laid everything out neatly and set my
alarm. Mom came in to help me into bed.
She propped me up on my side with pillows,
including a pillow between my knees to
keep them from getting a pressure sore.
Then she stroked my hair, switched off

the bedside lamp, and said good night.

I tried hard to go to sleep, but I lay awake. I could hear Monica brushing her teeth in the bathroom, and that made me wonder— were my parents and the principal *sure* I could fit into the restrooms at Jordan? And what if I couldn't? Mom and Dad wouldn't be around to help if I got stuck.

For what felt like an hour, I lay there wondering and worrying about a zillion things. Would I like my teachers? Would they like me? Would I make friends? Would I be in any of Chip or Mandy or even April's classes? Would I fit under the lunch tables? Would kids think I was retarded because I had to take Adaptive Physical Education classes instead of regular P.E.?

I thought about everything from the height of the lockers to the height of the library shelves. Finally, exhausted, I conked out. All night I dreamed I was wheeling myself to class on a conveyor belt that kept going backwards.

The next morning I got up early, though I hardly felt rested. Monica was in the shower. Josh was probably up organizing his backpack, even though Willowbrook Elementary didn't begin for another two hours. I could hear Mom in the kitchen scrambling eggs for breakfast and packing school lunches. Dad would be leaving for work soon. There was something very familiar about the morning routines, but I couldn't help thinking that everything felt different.

I wouldn't be riding on the bus with Mandy and Chip, and the others. Mom would be driving me to school, because the county didn't have a school bus with a mechanical lift. Already I could feel my stomach tighten as I pictured our old station wagon rumbling up to the front of Jordan Junior High and my mom getting out my wheelchair and transferring me out of the car—while scores of kids looked on.

Monica walked into my bedroom, towel-drying her hair. She helped me pull up my jeans and button them. "Ready for me to help you into your chair?"

After straightening my pant legs, she angled my wheelchair next to my bed. Then she lifted my legs as I grabbed the armrests and hoisted myself into the seat.

"Everything else within reach?" she said as she picked up her towel.

"You could hand me my Easter egg

sweater, thanks," I said as I pointed to my closet.

Monica slid the sweater off its hanger. "Excited about junior high?"

I didn't know how to tell her how nervous I was without making it sound like another Feel-Sorry-for-Darcy day. I decided I would try my best to be positive. "Yeah, I'm excited. Why not?"

"Because this will be the start of a whole new experience for you." She smiled as she reached into the pocket of her terrycloth robe and pulled out a delicate press-powder compact. "For you."

"What'll I do with this?" I said as I turned the thing over in my hands. "You and Mom use this stuff, not me."

"You will," Monica said in a sing-song way. "You'll see."

All the way to school that morning I kept thinking about what it would be like. I knew I was supposed to go directly to the principal's office so that he could show me around—describe where the ramps were and how to take short cuts to my classes. In one sense it was an honor to have an actual principal help me out, but on the other hand I didn't want it to look like I was getting

107

special attention. Would kids think it was cool to be seen with the principal? I wasn't sure.

When we pulled up to the campus, I was surprised to see how big and spread out the buildings were. I had passed by Jordan whenever my family went to my uncle's house, but it looked different now, surrounded by bunches of buses and a ton of teenagers.

Mom parked the station wagon behind the last bus in the school circle and got out my wheelchair. As she helped me into my chair, I glanced around. Kids streamed past me, but none of them stared outright. Most of them played the trick of looking out of the corners of their eyes, pretending not to notice. That's rude, but I don't really mind. I've looked at cute boys, even Chipper, that way when I haven't wanted them to notice my stares.

Still, I wished that kids wouldn't stare. It would be a lot better if they would just come out and say something, anything—like "Hey, where did you get such a wild-colored wheelchair?"

I felt a little left out, watching so many kids who looked like they knew where they were heading. I wasn't sure where I was going, but I decided not to listen to those feel-sorry feelings. I wedged my notebook between my leg and chair, waved to Mom, and headed inside.

"Darcy, don't you want me to go with you?" Mom called.

I swung around with as brave a smile as I could muster. "I've got it all under control, Mom. Just head for the principal's office, right?" It was important to me that I start off the first day by myself.

"Okay, honey. I'll be parked here at 3:00 to pick you up."

I fell in line behind a crowd of kids who were streaming through the front doors. Hanging across the foyer was a colorful banner reading, "Welcome Jordan Jaguars!" I veered to the left and found the principal's office, and a secretary told me to wait.

Soon a big man in a gray pinstriped suit opened the office door. He smiled warmly, introduced himself as Mr. Peck, and shook my hand. That was a switch. Not many adults had ever shook my hand before.

"Well, Miss DeAngelis, you are the first physically impaired student we've ever had here at Jordan," he said as he adjusted his glasses and flipped through what I guessed were my school records.

I liked the sound of that word, "student." I had to agree with April that some junior high words certainly came across better than elementary school words. "Student" had a nicer ring to it than "pupil." But I wasn't sure if I liked the privilege of being "first," and I certainly didn't like being referred to as "physically impaired." It made me sound like a nerd, all scientific and statistical. I preferred "disabled."

"Your parents and I have discussed your needs, and I think you'll fit in just fine."

He explained where my classes were and gave me a little map to follow. He said my teachers had prepared their classrooms, widening the aisles between the desks so I could wheel through. Maybe junior high wouldn't be too bad after all.

I spun out of the office and coasted past a brick wall with a big school emblem on it—a bronze jaguar with a lot of Latin written below it. The halls were overflowing with kids, a few of whom where also walking alone with their maps, I noticed.

"Hey Darcy, wait up!" a familiar voice

110

called out from behind me.

I spun around and spotted Chip, pushing his way through the crowd. Suddenly I wasn't nervous about school, I was nervous about him! He looked like he belonged in junior high—his new sweater and corduroys made him look like a full-fledged teenager. What should I say to him?

"I see you made it to school okay," he said, out of breath from running. "Mandy told me your mom was giving you a ride."

I blushed. "Yeah, I'm here. Now what?" I said good-naturedly, looking at my map to divert his attention to something else.

As we walked and wheeled down the hall, Chip and I compared schedules. We had the same Spanish class after lunch! He said maybe we could sit together, if the teacher didn't assign places. With that he socked my shoulder, said goodbye, and headed to his first class in the other direction.

I couldn't believe it—Chipper actually wanted to sit with me. *Man,* I thought, *this is turning out better than I imagined.*

I made a righthand turn into room 102, social sciences, and got my first taste of reality as a junior higher. The desks were awful—the desktops were connected to the seats, so I couldn't use my desk. The teacher, a stern-looking woman who wore her glasses on a chain around her neck, ordered me to sit in the back of the room and use the book table as a desk. It would be temporary, she explained, but that didn't help me today. I felt painfully different.

My second period literature class was on the second floor. *No problem*, I thought as I headed toward the elevator Mr. Peck had shown me. I punched the elevator button and waited. A full five minutes later, after the class bell had rung and the hall was clear of students, I was still pushing it. Finally a janitor walked by with a mop and explained that the elevator had broken down an hour earlier.

I fought back tears as I wheeled to Mr. Peck's office. He sent a runner up to my class to explain why I hadn't arrived and to retrieve my literature book and homework. How humiliating! Would this be a regular happening?

I pushed the thought out of my mind as I spent the class period in the office working on my social sciences homework. Homework—the first day of school?! This certainly wasn't Willowbrook Elementary.

The rest of the afternoon was nearly as disastrous. When the class bell rang, I headed toward my locker to put away my social science book. I felt sick—the locker was on the upper row, out of reach! I turned around and headed back to the principal's office.

I thought I was doing pretty well when I went to the restroom before lunch and was able to fit through the door. Sure enough, I could fit into the bathroom. But when I came out, my heart sank—the mirrors were all too high to see myself, and there was no way I could have wheeled through the mob of girls primping and preening, anyway.

I pretended it didn't bother me as I checked myself out in the little mirror of the compact Monica had given me. I stuffed it back in my pocketbook. Monica had meant it as a happy get-ready-for-the-boys gift. Little did she know I'd use it as a cover-up for being embarrassed.

At lunchtime I bumped into Mandy—I was so relieved that we shared the same lunch period! But she felt as bad as I did when we realized that I couldn't fit underneath the cafeteria tables. They all had those hooked-on benches. We took our lunch outside in the courtyard, where Mandy sat on a brick wall and I parked next to her.

"Boy, my math teacher is really fun . . . and I *love* science class. I think we're gonna actually cut up frogs and stuff," Mandy jabbered as she unwrapped her sandwich. "I've got Amy in my first period class and Jared in the second."

"You're kidding. I don't know anybody in my classes yet."

She took a bite. "I'm sorry, Darce. How's it going otherwise?"

"To be honest," I said, staring at my sandwich on my lap, "not so hot." I explained all that had happened. "But I'm not going to let it get me down."

"That's the spirit," Mandy said through a mouthful.

We compared schedules. No classes together.

With only lunch period in common, we would surely drift apart as friends. And eventually, I figured, Mandy would want to sit with her new friends at regular cafeteria tables. The thought made me sad.

I wrapped up my half-eaten sandwich. Lunch had ended up as another disaster.

14

The rest of the day was no better.

After lunch I headed toward Spanish class, hoping my nervousness wouldn't show. Again. I wasn't sure the knots in my stomach were due to the whole crazy day, or if I was just uptight about seeing Chipper.

It didn't matter. When I got to class, the teacher was in the middle of pointing us to our pre-arranged seats. Chipper was at the front of the room. My seat was all the way in the back at the opposite corner.

He waved his pencil at me.

That's when Senora Lopez slapped her desk with a ruler and rattled off a lot of

Spanish gibberish that none of us understood. I got the message that this was a no-nonsense class, and Chipper and I definitely would not get the chance to pal around.

Spanish class was the longest and most brain-taxing period of the day, and Senora Lopez kept us late. Everyone had to scurry extra fast for the next class, including Chipper, who got pushed out the front door before I had a chance to catch his eye.

I sighed, dropped my books onto my lap, and slowly wheeled out of the room. My last class of the day was just across the hall.

"Well, fancy meeting you here," I heard someone say. I glanced over my shoulder. It was April, dressed fit to kill and hobbling on her crutches.

"You still on those things?" I said, brightening a bit.

"This is the last week," she said as she wiped her forehead, pretending to be exhausted.

We straggled into the classroom, saying how glad we were to share a class. And to be honest, I truly *was* glad.

"Have you been able to get around okay?" I asked April as we chose two seats together near the back of the room.

"Not too bad," she shrugged. "Except the elevator broke down."

"Yeah, wasn't that the pits?!" I exclaimed happily. I had forgotten that somebody like April with a sprained ankle would have to use the elevator, too. Not that I wished her trouble getting to classes, too, but it felt good to have someone to identify with.

"Thankfully," she gushed, "Chipper and Paul just happened to be going up the stairs at that exact moment."

"Oh?"

"Yes. They helped me all the way up to the second floor!"

"Oh. That was nice," I said, feeling all the "oomph" go out of me. Another blow. The rest of math period was a blur as I tried very hard to concentrate on what the teacher was saying.

The last bell of my first day at school buzzed at exactly five minutes to three. Tired and a little overwhelmed, I wheeled in the direction of the new locker I had been assigned. I loaded everything into my backpack, slung it around my chair handles, and headed for the circle drive in front of the school.

The kids were a lot more rowdy and hang-

117

loose than they'd been coming in that morning. They laughed, threw wads of notebook paper at each other, and played with yo-yo's on their way to the buses.

I parked my wheelchair at the end of the last school bus in line and waited for our old station wagon. One by one, the long line of buses zoomed out of the circle, turning right or left. I spotted Bus #342, Mandy and Chipper's bus, as it pulled away. I strained, hoping they would look back and see me and wave. Mom was late.

The school circle was quiet now, except for a few walkers who passed by. A breeze stirred the trees around me, and I looked up into one of the bluest skies I had ever seen. Big, billowy clouds raced across the sky, and another breeze ruffled the leaves. I took a deep breath. This was one day I was glad to see end.

Just then I noticed a butterfly frolicking toward me from across the street. He flipped and danced in my direction. I cocked my head, staring at the butterfly as though it were the most curious thing I'd ever seen. Suddenly, all the lessons I had learned this last summer came flooding back. God was even in this day! I had forgotten that!

118

If I had learned anything over the summer, I had learned that Jesus specializes in answering prayer, sometimes in ways you would least expect. His answers, especially for me, are always different.

Different. I thought once again about my Dad's famous saying, "We all have handicaps!" And I thought back over the day, remembering a couple kids who were Asian . . . a girl in my math class who had more pimples than a Clearasil ad . . . a boy who sat in my row in social sciences who wore extra thick glasses . . . and scads of kids with full sets of braces on their teeth. Even too-tall Chipper stood at least a head above most of the kids in our Spanish class.

The butterfly danced a silly little jig in front of me and then flipped away as Mom and the station wagon pulled into the circle. Tears welled up in my eyes as I watched my butterfly friend flutter away.

God had remembered me. He had not left me or forsaken me. And tomorrow, I decided, would be an adventure. I would expect God to do something . . . different.

GLOSSARY

Here are a few words and expressions you met in *Darcy* that may have been new to you.

Accessible—A place that is easy to enter (steps and narrow doorways are a pain if you're in a wheelchair). Also, "accessible" to a blind person may mean that there are braille signs to help them find their way . . . like on an elevator. "Accessible" to a deaf person may mean that there is a sign language interpreter present or a TDD (telecommunication device for the deaf). The TDD allows a deaf person to type a message and send it over their phone line.

Ramp—Wheelchairs can't use steps! Also, curb-cuts fit into this category.

Disability—Any physical injury or illness that limits you from doing, seeing, or hearing things. Some people call a disability a "physical impairment."

Limitations—Being unable to do everything that other kids can do. We can be limited by our size, our strength, or even a pair of eye glasses with a strong prescription!

Handicap—Something that prevents a disabled person from being all that he can be or do. A curb will "handicap" a disabled person in a wheelchair.

Physically challenged—A fancy way of saying that you are disabled or handicapped. Some people invent other phrases like "motor impaired" or "handicapable" or "handicopable."

Paralyzed—A disabling condition in which parts of your body cannot move. Sometimes it means that person cannot feel, either. To be paralyzed does not mean that you are "stiff."

Pressure sore—A sore which occurs when a paralyzed person sits or lies in one position too long. It is very hard to heal, and disabled people take many precautions to prevent such sores from happening.

Adaptive P.E.—A physical education program in school which is modified to include someone who is disabled. Special games and exercises are devised for kids in wheelchairs.

Insecure—A feeling you get when you keep comparing yourself to others and come out on the losing end. Insecure kids tend to be either very shy or very bossy.

A Note from Joni

I know you'd get a kick out of helping someone like my friend Darcy. She's pretty special, isn't she? Can you imagine yourself pushing her wheelchair or helping her transfer from one seat to another?

In case you are looking for ways to help a friend who is disabled, I've got a list of suggestions to share. Roll up your sleeves, reach out, and share God's love with a friend who is disabled. You'll not only put a smile on his or her face, you'll end up smiling, too.

• Take some Windex or chrome cleaner, a rag, and a sponge, and shine up a friend's wheelchair. Grown-ups get their cars washed, waxed, and polished; why shouldn't kids in wheelchairs have a shiny set of wheels too?

• Learn how to push a wheelchair. There is more to it than simply throwing your weight behind the handlebars. Watch out for the cracks in the sidewalk or lips on the edge of the curb. Give a smooth, safe ride to a friend in a chair.

• Offer to be a reacher or a picker-upper.

Offer to reach for the top books on the library shelf, or pick up an item for him on the way to class. How about carrying an extra load of books if they don't fit on your friend's lap? Look around and discover ways you can help.

• When yakking with your friend in a wheelchair, be sure to stand in front and not off to the side or behind the chair. Then she won't have to constantly strain her neck to see what's going on.

• It's okay to ask your disabled friend about his handicapping condition, but remember that kids like to talk about lots of other things besides their chairs or crutches or hearing aids . . . like sports and games, TV shows, vacations, hobbies, and even homework—maybe!

• Ask your disabled friend if he has any prayer requests. Sometimes kids, whether they're disabled or able-bodied, feel lonely, wish their parents didn't fight so much, need somebody to pray for them, or just want to talk.

• Think ahead. If you're going to go somewhere with your disabled friend on the school campus, stop and think if there will be steps or a high curb. Will she be able to fit under the cafeteria table? If not, ask a teacher to help out. Remember, there is always a way if you've got the will!

Jon